Library of Congress Cataloging-in-Publication Data

Berlin, Irving, 1888–1989.
  White Christmas / by Irving Berlin ; illustrated by Michael Hague. — 1st ed.
    p. cm.
  Summary: An illustrated version of the popular Christmas song, with sheet music included in the back of the book.
  ISBN 978-0-06-029123-5 (trade bdg.) — ISBN 978-0-06-029124-2 (lib. bdg.)
  1. Children's songs, English — United States — Texts. 2. Christmas music — Texts. [1. Songs. 2. Christmas music.
3. Snow — Songs and music.] I. Hague, Michael, ill. II. Title.
PZ8.3.B4565Wh 2010
782.42'1723 — dc22

2009035133
CIP
AC

Music notation design by Matt Adamec
Typography by Jeanne L. Hogle
10 11 12 13 14 SCP 10 9 8 7 6 5 4 3 2 1
❖
First Edition

White Christmas

By Irving Berlin

Illustrated by Michael Hague

An Imprint of HarperCollinsPublishers

To Meghan and Adam
— M.H.

The sun is shining,
The grass is green,
The orange and palm trees sway.
There's never been such a day
In Beverly Hills, L.A.
But it's December the twenty-fourth,
And I am longing to be up north.

I'm dreaming of a white Christmas,

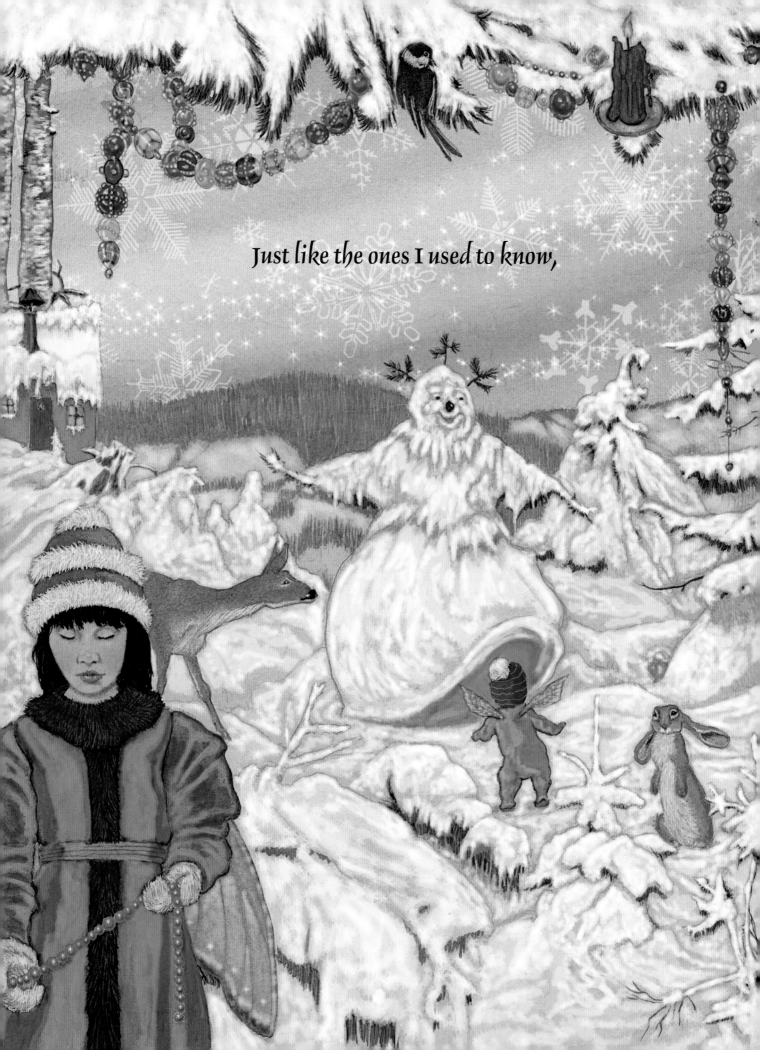

Just like the ones I used to know,

Where the treetops glisten

And children listen

To hear sleigh bells in the snow.

I'm dreaming of a white Christmas

With ev'ry Christmas card I write:

"May your days be merry and bright

And may all your Christmases be white."

White Christmas

words and music by Irving Berlin

The sun is shin - ing, the grass is green, ___ the

or - ange and palm trees sway. There's nev - er been such a day in